The Moccasins
written by Earl Einarson
illustrated by Julie Flett

THEYTUS BOOKS

Third printing, 2015
Library and Archives Canada Cataloguing in Publication

Einarson, Earl, 1962-
          The moccasins / written by Earl Einarson ; illustrated by Julie Flett.

ISBN 1-894778-14-6

1. Einarson, Earl, 1962- --Childhood and youth--Juvenile literature.
2. Native children--Canada--Juvenile literature. 3. Foster children--Canada--Juvenile literature. 4. Moccasins--Juve-
nile literature. 5. Native peoples--Canada--Ethnic identity--Juvenile literature. 6. Authors, Canadian (English)--21st
century--Biography--Juvenile literature. I. Flett, Julie II. Title.

PS8609.I53M62 2004   jC818'.609   C2004-903594-0

                              Printed in Canada

We acknowledge the support of the Canada Council for the Arts, which last year invested $157 million to
bring the arts to Canadians throughout the country. *Nous remercions le Conseil des arts du Canada de son
soutien. L'an dernier, le Conseil a investi 157 millions de dollars pour mettre de l'art dans la vie des Cana-
diennes et des Canadiens de tout le pays.* We acknowledge the support of the Province of British Columbia
through the British Columbia Arts Council

The Moccasins
by Earl Einarson

This book is dedicated to my foster mother Mildred and to all other foster
parents who give of themselves and provide love when it is most needed.

When I was young, my foster brothers and I slept together in one room. My bed was on the far end. I always waited until I heard them sleeping before I would fall asleep. I felt warm and loved.

My foster mother gave me moccasins to wear in the house. They were fine soft shoes made of tanned hide with a beaded pattern on top. She told me my background was Native, and that it was a good thing to be. She told me to wear my moccasins proudly. The hide smelled good, like a cozy campfire. They made me feel warm and loved.

I wore my moccasins every day. I put them on first thing in the morning and did not take them off until I went to bed with my brothers. When it rained, I played marbles on the kitchen floor wearing my moccasins. And, sometimes my foster mother would carry me to bed with my moccasins still on.

I wore my moccasins so much that I started to wear them out. My foster mother got a needle and buckskin, and sewed them back together. After a while, I grew and my moccasins did not fit me anymore. My foster mother said it was time to put them away. We put them in a box and packed them away

Later, I grew some more. I grew into a bigger boy and then into a man. I began my own family. The Creator blessed my family by bringing us a beautiful child.

When my baby was born, my foster mother brought a gift. It was a box. Inside the box were my old moccasins. I took them out and held them. The smell of the soft hide reminded me of how they used to make me feel warm and loved. I placed them carefully on a shelf above my baby's crib.

The box will stay on the shelf until my baby is big enough to fit those old moccasins. When I give him the moccasins, I will tell him of the love I had when I wore them. I will tell him how safe and loved I felt. I will tell him of how proud I am to be Native. When he puts those moccasins on, I know that he will feel proud too.